This book has been specially written and published
for World Book Day 2016. For further information,
visit **www.worldbookday.com**.
World Book Day in the UK and Ireland is made possible
by generous sponsorship from National Book Tokens,
participating publishers, authors, illustrators and booksellers.
Booksellers who accept the £1★ World Book Day Book
Token bear the full cost of redeeming it.

World Book Day, **World Book Night** and **Quick Reads**
are annual initiatives designed to encourage everyone in the
UK and Ireland – whatever your age – to read more and
discover the joy of books and reading for pleasure.

World Book Night is a celebration of books and reading
for adults and teens on 23 April, which sees book gifting and
celebrations in thousands of communities around the country:
www.worldbooknight.org

Quick Reads provides brilliant short new books
by bestselling authors to engage adults in reading:
www.quickreads.org.uk

★€1.50 in Ireland

This book is dedicated to anyone who struggles
with reading and writing. Dream big, fly high,
and never let anyone stop you.
Love, Cerrie
C.B.

For Charlie, my wonderful agent xxx
L.E.A.

First published in the UK in 2016 by Scholastic Children's Books
An imprint of Scholastic Ltd
Euston House, 24 Eversholt Street,
London, NW1 1DB, UK
Registered office: Westfield Road, Southam, Warwickshire, CV47 ORA
SCHOLASTIC and associated logos are trademarks and / or registered
trademarks of Scholastic Inc.

Text copyright © Cerrie Burnell, 2016
Illustrations copyright © Laura Ellen Anderson, 2016

The right of Cerrie Burnell to be identified as the author and
of Laura Ellen Anderson to be identified as the illustrator
has been asserted by them.

ISBN 978 1407 16605 6

A CIP catalogue record for this book is available from the British Library.

Printed and bound by CPI Group (UK) Ltd, Croydon, CRO 4YY

Papers used by Scholastic Children's Books are made
from wood grown in sustainable forests.

1 3 5 7 9 10 8 6 4 2

This is a work of fiction. Names, characters, places,
incidents and dialogues are products of the author's imagination
or are used fictitiously. Any resemblance to actual people, living
or dead, events or locales is entirely coincidental.

www.scholastic.co.uk

HARPER
AND THE
Sea of Secrets

CERRIE BURNELL
Illustrated by Laura Ellen Anderson

■SCHOLASTIC

Once there was a girl called Harper who had a rare musical gift. She heard songs on the wind, rhythms on the rain and hope in the beat of a butterfly's wing. Harper could play every instrument she touched, but her favourite of all was the harp. For whenever she played its silken strings, the air seemed to whisper with magic...

Chapter One
THE MESSENGER GULL

High on the topmost floor of the Tall Apartment Block, Harper was dreaming of music – a melody of stars and storms. Suddenly, a frantic squawking cut through the song, and her dream was full of feathers.

Harper opened a single sea-grey eye and peered through a gap in the velvety curtains. To her surprise a huge gull was hovering

outside. Its wings were the colour of the sea at dawn and its eyes were as sharp as flint. "You must have come from the sea," Harper breathed.

Elsie Caraham popped her head around the sitting-room door and gave a wild grin. "That, young Harper, is a messenger gull," she cried. "Look, it's carrying a message." Elsie Caraham was the oldest resident of the Tall Apartment Block. Harper was staying with her whilst her great aunt Sassy was away. If anyone knew anything about birds, it was Elsie, as she had lived near the skies all her life.

Harper seized her magical Scarlet Umbrella and ran out the door on to the rooftop, her pyjamas fluttering in the breeze. Exactly three paces behind her prowled Midnight, her beloved cat. In a matter of seconds, Harper

had flung the umbrella open, flipped it upside down, hopped inside with Midnight and was sailing up into the morning sky, towards the circling gull.

In the stormy air above the City of Clouds, the gull dived towards the Scarlet Umbrella. Harper closed her eyes and shivered as the great bird rushed past, dropping the letter into her hands. Then, with a parting squawk, the gull was gone, soaring away to a far-off sea.

Harper's fingers trembled with excitement. She very rarely got letters, and when she did, it was normally birthday cards or poems from her friend Ferdie. But this letter looked different. For a start, the envelope was purple and it smelled faintly of lavender. "I think it's from Great Aunt Sassy!" Harper called down to Elsie who was watching from the rooftop as she tore the envelope open. Inside was a map, a set of directions and a note scrawled in lavender ink:

HELP!

The orchestra I'm working with have all had their instruments STOLEN!

You must bring new ones from the Tall Apartment Block to the City of Gulls at once!

Without instruments the SONGS OF THE SEA festival will be cancelled, and all my precious costumes will go to waste.

PLEASE HURRY!

Love,
Great Aunt Sassy
x

With the gentlest of thoughts, Harper brought the Scarlet Umbrella floating back to the rooftop. Before it had even landed, she pulled her piccolo flute from her pocket and played three sharp notes. This was the secret signal that let her three best friends know she needed their help.

Moments later, there was a scuffling sound at the far end of the rooftop. Harper, Midnight and Elsie stared as a small tangled ball of hair emerged from amongst some plant pots. The hair could well have been a nest for a family of mice, or it could have belonged to a child.

"Liesel!" Harper cried as a small bright-eyed girl with scuffed knees and a muddy face scampered up to her.

Next came a swish of sleek fur, and a wolf the shade of morning mist slunk on to the rooftop. At the wolf's side was a boy who moved as

8

silently as moonlight, and although he could hardly see the world around him, he knew every street of the city: Nate Nathanielson.

Lastly came Ferdie, a serious boy with a serious scarf and a pencil tucked behind his ear, ready to write down stories.

The four children, the wolf and the cat all crowded around the letter.

"Sassy needs our help," said Harper.

"There's only one thing for it," cried Ferdie. "We need to gather every instrument we can and tie them to the Scarlet Umbrella!"

Nate gave a wide grin. "Yes, just like we did when we rescued the cats from the Midnight Orchestra."

Liesel gave a twirl of glee, skipped across the roof and rang a large silver bell. This was the Tall Apartment Block's meeting bell, which summoned every resident to the rooftop.

Within minutes a crowd had gathered. As soon as they heard the news of the stolen instruments they stumbled off sleepily, still in their dressing gowns, and returned with a splendid collection.

There was a huge and mighty double bass, a round, booming drum, a sparkling trombone, Madame Flora's cherry-wood piano, Harper's precious cello, Ferdie's button accordion, Liesel's silver triangle and Nate's brother's Roman tuba!

Elsie Caraham and Madame Flora took a strand of edentwine – an unbreakable string made from the stems of storm blooms – and set to work tying each instrument to the handle of the Scarlet Umbrella. Nate carefully attached a large kite and Midnight's cat basket. Ferdie took hold of the kite like a glider, and Liesel shot into the cat basket.

10

Harper scooped up Midnight, leaped into the upside-down umbrella, and helped Nate in after her. With a wondrous bound Smoke joined them, her golden eyes blazing like stars.

"Good luck," Elsie cheered, waving them off. Harper closed her eyes and, with a silent wish, commanded the Scarlet Umbrella to take them into the sky. Up they soared, up high above the City of Clouds, four children, a cat, a wolf and a trail of magnificent instruments, gleaming in the morning rain.

They were on their way to City of Gulls. They were on their way to adventure.

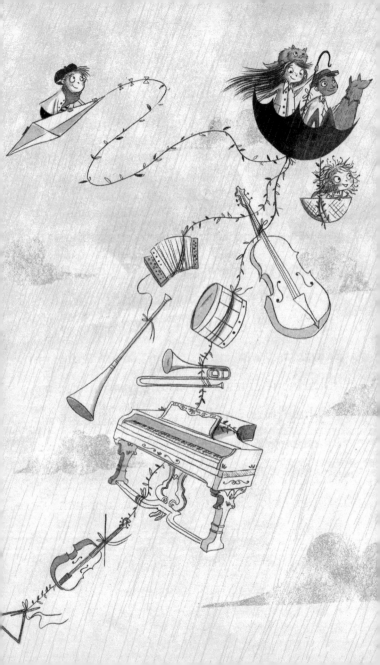

Chapter Two
THE CITY OF GULLS

"Follow the river north!" yelled Ferdie, studying the map in his hands.

"Got it," called Nate, reaching out over the side of the Scarlet Umbrella and feeling through cloudburst rain and a patch of thunder.

Liesel peered down from the cat basket and gave a scream of excitement when the

river roared into view.

"Which way now?" asked Harper.

"Follow the river to the foot of the Mist Mountain, then turn left and pick up the scent of the sea," cried Ferdie.

"OK," Harper smiled. As the peak of Mist Mountain loomed into sight, she helped Nate steer the Scarlet Umbrella left, then whispered to it, "Take us to the sea." At once, the sharp scent of salt tickled their noses. Then the clouds thinned and the children gasped.

You see, in the City of Clouds there are six types of rain that fall, float and patter from the sky every single day, in many different ways. Rain is what the children knew, and rain was the weather they loved the best. But as the Scarlet Umbrella carried them far from home, they were each struck by golden-bright sunshine. Harper laughed in

14

amazement, and Ferdie quickly loosened his scarf. He much preferred cold, lonely greyness.

Nate smiled and took off his hat, and Liesel leaped and turned a perfect pirouette in the cat basket.

A wild sea-wind snatched up the Scarlet Umbrella as if it were a fallen leaf. The children whooped and clung on tightly as they soared towards the City of Gulls, the instruments clanging and banging and sending odd notes of music tumbling down into the day.

"The City Gulls!" Liesel squealed as thousands of soaring birds came into sight." But it was not just gulls that swooped through the sky. Seabirds of every type were circling the green waters, their wings spread wide, their eyes seeking out silvery fish.

Smoke sat up straight, her nose tipped

towards where the moon might be, howling with happiness and hope. Nate laughed and ruffled her fur.

Harper noticed that the city itself was a peculiar little place, full of winding lanes and quaint old shops selling ships in bottles or deep-sea treasures. Instead of thick cloud the air was full of light, and the cry of the gulls rang through the streets.

She shivered with excitement. There was definitely a sense of mystery to this place.

Above her, Ferdie peered down from his kite. "The rooftops here look haunted," he murmured, deciding at once that he liked City of Gulls very much. It looked like the kind of place old explorers might live in. Ferdie pulled his pencil from behind his ear and began scribbling a sea-shanty.

"Look, there's an old crumbling pier," said

Liesel, quickly describing it for Nate. "It's a strange old structure that's half fallen into the sea."

"There's no sand on the beach," added Harper, "just a shore of pale white pebbles and sea of swirling green."

Nate listened happily. He could make out the dazzling glitter of the water, like a shadow edged in starlight, and he could feel the kiss of salt on his skin.

As they swooped down over the beach, they saw a bandstand and the Royal Seaside Pavilion. Gathered upon the bandstand was an orchestra of musicians without a single instrument, all miming the notes they should have been playing.

"What are they doing?" asked Ferdie.

"Pretending to play imaginary instruments," said Harper sadly.

"Perhaps they'll cheer up now we've brought them some real ones," Nate grinned. But he could not have been more wrong. For no sooner had Great Aunt Sassy come running out of the Seaside Pavilion and carefully helped the children lower each instrument on to the bandstand, than the entire orchestra started moaning. And what a terrible fuss they made! Harper had never heard such a racket.

"We can't possibly play this drum, it's not loud enough!" huffed a large ruby-cheeked man whose voice seemed to boom.

"And I simply cannot play this cello, it's too old," declared a graceful woman with curvy dark hair.

"This double bass is not acceptable," piped up a tall man with sturdy shoulders.

"Well, this piano is out of tune," complained

19

a red-haired woman with a fretful frown.

Liesel scowled at the woman crossly. "Perhaps you just don't know how to play it," she said, with a toss of her messy curls.

The orchestra glared at the small girl angrily, their eighty pairs of eyes staring hard. Ferdie stood up taller – he was ready to stick up for his sister. Great Aunt Sassy flapped her arms anxiously, and turned round and round like a confused duck.

Smoke gave a low forewarning growl and the orchestra all took a huge step back. At once Nate's hand was on the wolf's head, soothing her mood. That was the wonderful thing about Smoke: she wasn't wild, but nor was she tame. Her heart was filled with loyalty for Nate. Yet with time, Smoke had grown very fond of Nate's friends – especially light-footed Liesel.

Nate softly stepped forward. "Listen," he said calmly to the orchestra. "There's no need to get upset. We just wanted to help with Songs of the Sea Festival. If you won't play the music, then Harper could instead." Nate turned his face towards his friend and beamed. For although he couldn't see her, he saw the outline of a girl who shimmered with harmonies, and he winked, making Harper smile.

Midnight tiptoed over to the cherry-wood piano and began tuning the notes with his tail. The orchestra stared with astonishment as Harper kissed Midnight's nose, then sat down to play. Each ivory key she touched seemed to fill the air with tunes that echoed of water and waves.

She moved on to the cello, followed by the double bass, drum and then the glistening trombone, with which she played three sharp notes. The others knew what to do. Ferdie began squeezing the button accordion, Liesel let the silver triangle ring out and Nate went wild on the Roman tuba, whilst Midnight and Smoke played a duet on Harper's cello.

By the end of the performance, the orchestra all looked quite sheepish. They muttered an apology and quickly went

22

back to miming the notes. Harper sighed. "They're still cross they've lost their own instruments."

"Well," said Ferdie in a serious tone, "unless we want to put up with more bad moods, we better try and find the missing instruments."

The others all gave a nod.

"Yes," agreed Nate, "let's split up."

Chapter Three
THE SMUGGLERS' MAP

Harper and Ferdie set off into the heart of the City of Gulls at a run. The city felt as odd as it had looked. Everything was slightly crooked, so neither of them could tell if they were walking up a hill or stumbling down a ditch.

Midnight, who normally tiptoed three paces behind Harper, scampered lightly in

front and darted through the doorway of a higgledy-piggledy shop. It was called "The Pirate's Pearl". The two children rushed after Midnight, but the little shop was packed so full of junk they had to climb over a massive barrel of rum and crawl beneath a three-legged table just to get inside.

Midnight sprang on to an old oak cabinet, knocking over a long wooden tube with a swish of his white-tipped tail. "Watch out," cried Ferdie, leaping to catch it.

The lid of the tube popped open and a faded sheet of parchment slipped to the floor. "What is it?" asked Harper as Ferdie carefully unfolded it.

"It's a map of underground passageways," Ferdie grinned, "all leading to the same place: Gull Island."

"What's Gull Island?" asked Harper.

"It's an old smuggler's hideout, just off the coast," echoed a voice croaky with sleep.

Harper and Ferdie spun around to see an old man sitting in a rocking chair. His eyebrows were snow-coloured, and he looked like he'd been snoozing for the last hundred years.

The old man winked a bright blue eye and gave a big crinkly smile before stumbling to his feet and saying in grand voice, "Ahoy, there! I'm Slim Joe, owner of the Pirate's Pearl and expert on the City of Gulls. What can I do for you?"

"We're looking for stolen instruments," said Ferdie.

Slim Joe gave a wise chuckle. "This city is built upon secrets," he said mysteriously.

Harper smiled. She knew there was something special about this place, and she could feel it under her feet.

"It's a smugglers' town, you see," Slim Joe went on. "Beneath the streets is indeed a maze of tunnels that lead out under the sea."

Both children gave a gasp of delight.

"Of course nobody uses the tunnels any more," said Slim Joe, pouring three cups of tea from a rusty old kettle.

"Why not?" asked Harper.

"Nobody knows the way in," Slim Joe shrugged.

"But doesn't it say on the map?" asked Ferdie.

Slim Joe shook his head. "The map marks all the tunnels, but it got torn, and now no one knows where the entrance is."

Ferdie gulped down a swig of bitter tea.

"We'll take the map," he cried, tightening his scarf.

"Consider it a gift," beamed Slim Joe.

"I wonder what other secrets this town holds," said Harper quietly.

"Well, plenty of folk say they hear songs coming from the waves. It's not called Sea of Secrets for nothing," mumbled Slim Joe.

Harper's eyes widened. "Come on," she cried, "we've got to get back to the beach."

Slim Joe watched in stunned silence as the two children ran into the street, scooped up Midnight, opened the Scarlet Umbrella and raced into the air. Soon their feet were skimming the rooftops as they flew through soaring gulls.

On the stony shores of the Sea of Secrets, Liesel and Nate wandered towards the

crumbling pier. Liesel danced ahead, her feet hardly touching the stones. Nate took in every crunch of every pebble, every fizz of every wave, every screech of every gull that looped the sky.

He loved it, and so did Smoke. There was a wildness in her step that Nate had only known her use at night. She was a blur of mist, a shadow with a heartbeat, streaking in and out of the waves, her fur turned silver with salt.

Then the wolf stopped, her ears pricked. She was picking up a sound that Nate couldn't hear. Liesel, who knew Smoke well, scurried over.

"Can you see anything strange?" asked Nate.

Liesel scanned the horizon, her small eyes beady as a gull's. "There's nothing but a boat

full of fishermen," she shrugged.

"Oh," smiled Nate. "Maybe Smoke can hear them singing." For the fishermen were all singing a lullaby of some sort.

But, as Liesel watched the beautiful wolf, she noticed Smoke was staring at the waves beyond. "Wait," she said, yanking Nate's sleeve. "I think Smoke's listening to something in the sea."

The children froze as, ever so faintly, the sound of music came drifting up from the pale green waves.

Chapter Four

THE BOAT OF BEARDY FISHERMEN

It didn't take Liesel long to find an abandoned rowing boat. With a wild splash and a nudge from Smoke, she got the boat into the water. Nate, who had never been in a boat before, clambered in and grabbed the two wooden oars in the bottom. With the wolf yapping at his side and Liesel sitting at the front, he began to steadily row. Soon they were out of icy shallows and close to the boat of beardy

fishermen. But the fishermen weren't taking any notice. Nate wasn't going to stand for his friend being ignored. He raised the Roman tuba to his lips and blew it like a foghorn.

The fishermen leaped like startled frogs. One fell into a bucket of eels, one almost toppled overboard, whilst another clung to the boat's white sail in terror. Then they spotted the two children and scowled. Nate couldn't see the fishermen clearly, but he could tell that they were men who had very big beards and that they moved as quickly as cats.

"We heard songs coming from the sea," Liesel yelled.

"Nothing to do with us, Miss," grumbled a fisherman with a telescope.

"They say the seas are haunted," chimed in another, who was holding a pipe.

33

"Might be your imagination," mumbled a third with a lot of tattoos.

Liesel frowned fiercely. "Wait here," she whispered to Nate, and before anyone could stop her, she sprang from wthe rowing boat and landed aboard the fishermen's boat.

Nate laughed as he realized what was happening and Liesel began to climb the sail, her

heart beating fast with joy. The fishermen cried out in anger, shaking their fists and bellowing. Though they were quick as cats, Liesel was quick as a mouse, and she reached the top of the mast in no time. You see, Liesel was a girl who dreamed of dancing with pirates and swimming with sharp-finned sharks. This beardy band of fishermen didn't scare her at all.

From the top of the sail she spotted a young boy who wasn't much older than Nate, and she beckoned to him. The boy, whose hair was fiery red, climbed the sail and, when no one was watching, he whispered to Liesel, "Take no notice of them."

"I won't," she grinned. "My name's Liesel. Who are you?"

"Samson," replied the boy. "This is my mum's boat, I keep an eye on it for her while

she's selling fish at the market." Then he added secretively, "These waters are wild and the sea is full of strange sounds."

Liesel's eyes twinkled. "So we *did* hear music!"

The boy nodded, and then stared down at the shore and frowned. Leisel quickly followed his gaze, and for a moment she thought she saw a woman at the end of the pier, with sunset hair and a beautiful cello. "You know, you might want to get off the boat before we dock," said Samson hurriedly. "Why?" asked Liesel. Samson shrugged and fidgeted. "It's just my mum might get

cross if she finds out I let you on to the boat."

"Is that your mum?" asked Liesel, pointing back to the shore – but the woman and the cello had disappeared. She pulled a tuneless recorder from her pocket and played three sharp notes. There was a faint whooshing sound, and Samson gasped as an umbrella of stunning scarlet silk descended from the clouds.

"Grab on," Ferdie yelled, reaching out to his sister. With a quick wave to Samson and the speechless fisherman below, Liesel leaped into her brother's arms, and away they all soared back to the beach, sweeping up Nate and Smoke as they went.

The tide was going out fast and, as they reached the pebbles, the children noticed that all along the crumbling pier children were perched with fishing lines, happily catching

crabs. Nate had never touched a crab before. Ferdie stayed with Smoke so she didn't munch all the bait. Harper led Nate up on to the pier and Midnight reached out a long claw, plucking a small red crab from a bucket for Nate.

Liesel did what a mouse might do: she darted and scampered along the pier until she reached the very end, where she crouched down low and gazed at the lapping sea. There below her, wading through the water, was Samson, the fiery-haired boy from the boat.

Liesel was about to call out when a seagull swooped from the air, trying to peck a piece of bacon. Liesel shooed it away. When she looked back, Samson was gone. Nowhere to be seen. He seemed to have vanished into the soft sea air.

Chapter Five

A LULLABY OF LOST SHIPS

Twilight fell across the City of Gulls and the sea turned fish-scale grey. "It's odd that everyone here is so grumpy," said Nate as they wandered back to the Seaside Pavilion.

"But not Slim Joe!" beamed Ferdie, pulling out the piece of parchment and showing it to his friends. "It's a map of all the tunnels

below the city. They all lead to the same place: Gull Island."

"Wow," breathed Nate, feeling the edges. He could always tell how old a note or letter was by the amount of creases that crossed it. This map was very old indeed.

Just then Great Aunt Sassy came tearing out of the doors of the Seaside Pavilion. "Harper, there you are, my love!" she cooed, giving her a warm hug. "Do go inside – we're in room seven. There are plenty of beds for all."

The children gazed at the bundle of splendid costumes billowing in Sassy's arms. "These precious outfits are for the festival – if we can find the instruments," Sassy sighed. Harper spotted a bright blue scarf, Liesel eyed a wondrous purple cloak, Ferdie admired a rather stylish tweed jacket and Nate felt the whisper of velvet.

"Well, I'd better deliver them to the orchestra just the same," Sassy smiled. With a swish of lavender silk, she was gone, sweeping down the stairs and into the evening mist.

The children dashed inside and found

room seven, which was indeed full of beds! There was a bunk bed, a queen's bed, a sofa bed, a hammock, a basket, a camp bed and a very bouncy waterbed. The most remarkable thing about the waterbed was that curled up happily in the middle of it was Midnight!

How he got into the room, or knew which bed Harper might choose, was a mystery. You see, Midnight was a most unusual cat. He seemed to know more about Harper than she did herself, sometimes prowling three steps behind, other times appearing at the very place she was supposed to be.

Harper curled up next to him, stroking his nightshade fur. "You're my best friend," she whispered.

Ferdie swung from the bunk to the sofa, before deciding the hammock was the perfect poet's nest. Liesel at once curled up in the

42

basket, much like a tired little mouse. Nate and Smoke settled eagerly down in the camp bed, the wolf becoming a pillow of claws and tail.

The moon cast bold shadows, and the children, the cat and the wolf drifted into a deep and wondrous slumber.

In her dream, Harper was lying upon the double bass, plucking its fine strings as it floated out to sea. All around her, stars reflected on the surf, dancing and glimmering to the tune she played: a shanty of salt and sorrows that whispered of wonder and waves.

Then suddenly there was howling and meowing, and someone was shaking her awake. "Harper, the sea is singing!" Ferdie cried.

Harper blinked her tired eyes and found that she wasn't playing the double bass

or sailing out to sea. She was lying on the waterbed, and the glorious song from her dream was echoing up from the beach.

Smoke and Midnight led the way out of their room and down to the beach where the children gathered listening to a song as mysterious as the moon that shimmered on the far-off waves. "If only we could reach the sea," sighed Harper.

Nate sniffed the dry salty air and shook his head. "Tide's too far out," he said.

"And it's too dark to see anything," Ferdie frowned.

"Not if you have these," came a voice through the moonlight.

The children turned to see Great Aunt Sassy leaning dramatically against the cherry-wood piano, clutching an armful of tiny lanterns, which flickered like fairy lights.

Around her were all the instruments they had brought from the Tall Apartment Block. At once Harper knew what they needed to do. "Grab an instrument," she cried, "Great Aunt Sassy, follow me to the sea!"

A little while later, Harper and Midnight were sitting in the Scarlet Umbrella, gently guiding it across silver-bright waves, towing her friends behind in a procession of music and love.

First came Ferdie, Nate and golden-eyed Smoke, riding upon the double bass. Next bobbed Liesel, tucked perfectly into the end of an upturned French horn. Lastly came Great Aunt Sassy, squashed inside a bass drum, her lavender petticoats billowing in the breeze.

Water lapped softly around them, strings twanged and the children giggled. Then the

song of the sea took hold of them and no one dared speak.

The music was just like in Harper's dream: a lullaby of lost ships with murmurs of mermaids.

For Ferdie, it was poetry. He grabbed his pencil and began scrawling words to sing to the tune.

For Liesel, it was energy, a tug at her toes that she couldn't ignore. She rose out of the French horn and twirled around upon its edge, like a marvellous midnight flamingo.

For Nate, it was stillness and beauty, a splendour that gripped him with joy.

For Sassy, it was a dream of costumes yet to come.

And for Harper, the melody was many things, but most of all it was love. She leaned over the edge of the Scarlet Umbrella, trying

to follow the sound, and gasped. "It's not just music," she breathed. "There are lights too."

The others peered down into the darkening sea and felt their hearts leap. Deep beneath the surface, glowing flecks of light flared like fallen stars. "It's like a rainbow at the bottom of the ocean," Ferdie whispered.

Nate smiled, for though he couldn't see the lights, he could sense his friends' amazement. "Where do you think it's coming from?" he whispered back.

Ferdie pulled the map of the smugglers' tunnels from his pocket and studied it by moonlight. "Perhaps someone is smuggling the instruments to Gull Island," he yelled.

They all stared through the dark in the direction of Gull Island, and sure enough, there in the distance, like stars shrouded in mist, was a light.

"Let's go there now," cried Harper, but Great Aunt Sassy softly cleared her throat.

"Darlings, it's awfully late and simply too far to sail to."

The children, who were shivering and actually couldn't stop yawning, knew deep down that Sassy was right. "If only we knew where the entrance to the tunnels was," Ferdie sighed crossly.

Liesel sat very still in her trombone. She thought of Samson, and how he seemed to have vanished into the sea. In the glow of the moon, she smiled. If anyone was mischievous enough to find a secret door, she was.

"Leave it to me," she chuckled.

Chapter Six
THE SECRET TUNNEL

When the soft pink light of dawn spread across the City of Gulls, Liesel was already awake. In fact, she was boinging up and down between the different beds, trying to get everyone's attention. "Come on, come on – I've found the entrance to the smugglers' tunnel!"

This got everybody out of bed pretty quickly – apart from Great Aunt Sassy, who

was wrapped in a shroud of sheets, snoring loudly.

The children crept outside, then ran like the wind to the crumbling pier. "How did you find it?" called Harper.

"I snuck out with Smoke and Midnight as soon as the sun rose and discovered it behind a rock," Liesel said, plunging knee-deep into icy water and wading to the end of the pier.

The others followed and, sure enough, cut into the rock behind a thick clump of black seaweed, was a door.

"Ta-dah!" Liesel yelled, jumping almost as high as the pier. She tried to wrench it open, and her face fell. It was locked.

Harper fumbled in her pocket and pulled out a hairpin. She handed it to Nate with a hopeful grin. "Will this do?"

Nate, who could open any door without

a key, set about trying to pick the lock. But the pin snapped. The lock wouldn't budge. "I need something bigger, something sharper," he mumbled.

Without any warning, Midnight leaped out of Harper's arms and swiped something red from the cold water. It was the shell of lobster claw.

"Good boy," beamed Nate as he slotted the claw carefully into the lock. With a loud groaning sound, the lock popped open and the door swung wide.

"Everyone inside," yelled Ferdie, and once they were all safely through the door, he yanked it shut behind them.

Suddenly the children were in utter blackness — somewhere very damp that smelled of rust and fishbones. For a moment Midnight's eyes held the light of the sun,

showing the children they were in a small leaky tunnel.

Then Midnight blinked and they were in darkness once again. But the children were not afraid. They knew that Nate was a boy of many talents, and one of them was that he could walk through the darkness just as easily as if it was day.

"Hold hands," he said gently, shuffling to the front of the line. Smoke walked proudly at her master's side while Nate guided the others further into the dark. Then boy and wolf stopped still. "The tunnel splits into two," said Nate. "Which one should we take?"

Nobody knew what to do. Harper closed her eyes and thought hard, and that was when she heard a sound. Not a loud sound, nor a long sound, but a sound that was full of light.

It was a single note played on the instrument Harper knew best.

"This way," she said, stumbling forwards and leading her friends to the left, for she was certain that at the end of the tunnel, someone was playing the harp. And she was right.

The four salt-skinned children, the cat and the wolf burst from the tunnel on to a beach of golden sand in a hidden cove on Gull Island.

Smoke gave an angry snarl, her fur standing up on end. Midnight leaped on to Harper's shoulders and the children stopped still. In front of them stood a bunch of beardy fishermen, each clutching an instrument like a weapon of war.

Harper stepped forward and gave them a smile. "I think you might have something that belongs to the orchestra," she said coolly.

Chaos broke out and the fishermen all

57

started shouting and stamping, but Harper held their gaze. You see, she had had to face other musicians far more terrifying than this seafaring band.

"Well, finders keepers. They're ours now," jeered the fisherman with the pipe.

"But why do you need them?" cried Ferdie.

"Do you know how to play?" added Nate.

The fishermen fidgeted uncomfortably, then from the middle of them stepped a woman with fiery red hair. She was as fierce and as beautiful as a storm at sea.

"Who are you?" spluttered Ferdie, who was in secret awe of this pirate-like woman.

Liesel stared at the woman's fiery hair and knew exactly who she was. "You're Samson's mum, aren't you?" she smiled.

The woman's face softened, "I am, lassie. My name's Una."

"Well, can you please tell us what's going on?" demanded Liesel.

Una, to everyone's surprise, said nothing. Instead, she picked up a fiddle and began to merrily play. She did not play it gracefully, or smoothly, or softly. She played it as if her soul was on fire, leaping around like a wild bird. The sound she made was astonishing.

Harper held her breath, and as the tune danced into her heart, she thought of the orchestra and their fabulous costumes. Then she pictured the grumpy fishermen who spent every day at sea, learning lullabies of lost ships and the wonders of the waves, and all at once she understood. She opened her eyes and spoke. "You are the ones who know the real *Songs of the Sea,* aren't you?"

The fishermen nodded solemnly.

"That's right, lassie," said Una. "We all play an instrument of some sort — be it a drum or crab basket. And we're right fed up of the orchestra taking over our festival."

Ferdie stood up straighter. He was a serious boy with a serious scarf, and he'd just had a seriously good idea. "What if we lent you some other instruments?" he suggested. "Then would you give these ones back?"

There was a lot of muttering and whispering. "How many instruments you got?" asked the fisherman with the telescope.

"Not enough," said Nate, listening to the many mumbling voices.

"I could always play my clam-organ," came a small voice from the back.

Everyone turned to see a boy with the same flame-red hair as Una holding up a set of clam-shells. "Samson!" Liesel grinned.

With a swift wink from Una, Samson started playing the clams like a mini mouth organ. The sound was shrill and funny, like the rushing of water over stones. It gave Harper a wonderful idea. She picked up a large pink shell and blew it like a horn. "If we could find enough shells I could teach you how to be the first-ever seashell band!"

Chapter Seven
THE SONGS OF THE SEA FESTIVAL

Almost at once a collection of seashells appeared on the golden sand. There was a huge grey shell almost bigger than Liesel that Samson and Ferdie strung fishing wire across, turning it into a cello – or *shello*.

There was a bundle of mussel shells which could be played like a glockenspiel. There were larger shells that formed fishing-wire

fiddles and a chorus of conches that could be played like flutes.

Harper found the fishermen were all excellent learners, and they knew the songs of the sea by heart. When the sun cast midday shadows, the band of beards were ready for the festival.

"Was it you playing last night in the tunnels below the sea?" asked Nate as they boarded the boat to sail back to the City of Gulls. The fishermen all chuckled and shook their heads.

"No," said the man covered in tattoos. "Nobody knows who plays those strange songs."

Liesel, who was perched at the top of the sail with Samson, gazed at the sea. It was as still as ice. Then, just for a second, she saw the surface break, and something strange and

mythical rose out of the water. "I saw a sea dragon!" she gasped.

Everyone ran to the edge of the boat. Ferdie seized a telescope and squinted through the lens, then almost dropped it in surprise. "Wow," he stuttered. "It's not a sea dragon ... it's a whale."

Una shook her head. "There aren't any such beasts in these waters any more."

But her son Samson spoke up. "There are, Mum. They've come back. I see them sometimes when I'm night fishing. There are dolphins, too. They're pretty shy, but if you play music, they come closer."

The fishermen all turned to stare at Harper, their eyes now twinkling with hope.

"Would you play something, lass?" asked Una.

Harper's face lit up in a smile. With the

help of Ferdie and Nate, she opened the Scarlet Umbrella, lowered it over the edge of the boat and stepped in. From deep within the umbrella's folds, Harper pulled a small, very old golden harp and started to softly play.

Her fingers found the notes of the tune from her dream: a harmony of sailors' hearts all singing their love to the seas.

Ever so slowly, all around her, the surf began to glow. At first, there was just a glimpse of dazzling turquoise, then a flash of bright jade, followed by bursts of pink and orange. A chorus of tails broke the surface, and shooting air rose from the waves.

"The whales are coming!" Liesel gasped. And they were. A school of legend-like mammals made a ring around the Scarlet Umbrella.

Harper kept playing as more and more sea

creatures came to join the song. There were bright-eyed dolphins and grey-skinned seals, glittering starfish and an inky octopus.

Harper stood up, with Midnight prowling elegantly along the rim of the umbrella. "Right," she called to the fishermen, "who's ready to put on a show?"

When three o'clock came in the City of Gulls, the orchestra's instruments had been returned to the bandstand, much to their great relief. The musicians all looked fantastic in Great Aunt Sassy's gorgeous gowns.

Amongst the cheerful audience sat Ferdie, Liesel and Nate, each of them giddy with excitement.

Smoke pricked her ears as the orchestra began to play. It was a stunning performance,

made up of tender melodies and tunes of moondust.

Just as the show came to an end, a new sound reached everyone's ears: the sound of a girl playing a solo on a strange old harp in the middle of the sea. Colours began flickering under the water, and a harmony echoed up from the waves.

Then there came a clapping of clamshells and a banging of baskets as a boat with white sails floated into view. On board, the band of beards raised their shells into the air and began to play for all they were worth – songs of patch-eyed pirates and shanties of sharp-toothed sharks.

The audience were spellbound. As Harper played on, gulls began to swarm in time to the beat, and the orchestra, enchanted by happiness, grabbed bows and horns and joined in.

The bandstand, the waters and the skies were alive with songs of the seas, all of them following the girl with the harp. The three children and Great Aunt Sassy could not have been prouder. Ferdie leaped up and grabbed the button accordion. Liesel joined in on the triangle, and Nate tooted away on the Roman tuba as if he'd been born on a boat.

It was the best Songs of the Sea Festival the City of Gulls had ever known. The fishermen, the orchestra and everyone in the town could finally be friends.

Later that evening, when the sun had set into the Sea of Secrets and the whales and sea creatures had all swum away, diving down deep to a world of blue, Una put her arms around Harper and thanked her. "You rescued the festival and made it what it should have always been," she said gently.

Harper smiled, "It wasn't just me. I couldn't have done it without my friends – or without Samson."

Una ruffled each of the children's sand-filled hair. "You're welcome to sail with us any time," she beamed.

Liesel's eyes lit up like sparklers and Ferdie had to hold her hand to stop her jumping aboard the boat right away. Nate gave a sailor's salute and, through the first rays of twilight, he could just make out a band of beardy fishermen grandly saluting back.

The children waved, Smoke howled, Midnight mewed a proud meow, and Samson called goodbye, then the boat with white sails was gone.

Great Aunt Sassy threw her arms around the four children. "You really saved the day!" she gushed, and because she was in a very

good mood, she added, "Shall we go out on the sea once more to hear the whales sing?" The children glowed with joy.

So the instruments were strung together and the girl with a harp towed out her friends in her enchanted umbrella. Behind her, the boy who knew the dark like the day smiled at his wolf. Beside him, on the double bass, a boy with a poet's heart pulled his pencil from behind his ear and got ready to write. And a little way off, a girl who dreamed of dancing with pirates imagined herself on a sea-bound adventure.

Great Aunt Sassy gazed up at the silver stars. Tomorrow they would travel back to the City of Clouds, but tonight was all about the sea. As it lapped softly around the instruments, the waters began to sparkle and the whale song began.

The children bobbed closer together and held hands. Far off on the midnight waters, like a ghost beneath the moon, sailed a ship with white sails, clanging out the songs of the sea upon shells. The children laughed – the band of beards was playing again.

"I hope we come back here," yawned Liesel, as they headed back to shore.

"We should come on a hot summer's day," smiled Nate, who was really rather tired.

"Then we could swim and join the dolphins," grinned Ferdie.

"And sing with the whales," sighed Harper, her eyes beginning to close.

Even though they had the choice of many lovely beds up at the Pavilion, the children decided to sleep on the bandstand, curled up on their instruments, gazing out at the starry sea.

"Sweet dreams, Midnight," Harper whispered, snuggling down beneath the Scarlet Umbrella, and listening to the lull of the waves. Midnight winked a green eye at her and twitched his ears. He took a last look at the glittering water and nestled under Harper's chin.

In her dreams, Harper was sailing in a boat with sails of scarlet silk, playing a small golden harp. From the waves she heard music — a song as old as time and wise as oceans — and she knew that one day they would all come back and learn more of the secrets of the sea.

Also look out for . . .

HARPER
AND THE
Scarlet
Umbrella

CERRIE BURNELL
Illustrated by Laura Ellen Anderson

When every single cat in the City of Clouds goes missing, Harper is determined to find her beloved Midnight and all the other precious pets.

Harper can't believe her luck when she discovers a magic flying umbrella and with the help of all her friends she sets off on a rescue adventure.

But they're up against the powerful Wild Conductor… Will they manage to bring the cats home?

HARPER
AND THE
Circus of Dreams

Cerrie Burnell

HARPER
AND THE
Circus of Dreams

ILLUSTRATED BY LAURA ELLEN ANDERSON

Late one evening as the stars begin to twinkle, Harper and her friends are flying on her magical Scarlet Umbrella when they see a girl running on air, skipping along a tightrope. She leads them to the wondrous Circus of Dreams, suspended in the clouds by hot-air balloons.

As the children meet the mermaid acrobat, the circus baker, the puzzling fortune teller and the acrobatics troop, they begin to realise something about Harper's mysterious past…

Cerrie Burnell is a presenter and writer, best known for her work in children's TV, and she featured in the *Guardian*'s 2011 list of 100 most inspirational women. Her other titles in this same series include *Harper and the Scarlet Umbrella* and *Harper and the Circus of Dreams*.

Laura Ellen Anderson is the incredibly talented illustrator of the *John Smith Is Not Boring* series and The *Witch Wars* series, as well as all the other *Harper* titles.

Picture books by the same creators:

Every snowflake is different,
every snowflake is perfect.

Snowflakes

Cerrie Burnell   Laura Ellen Anderson

Mermaid

Cerrie Burnell
Laura Ellen Anderson

Ballet Dreams

Cerrie Burnell & Laura Ellen Anderson

If you enjoy magical stories, also look out for Bella Broomstick by Lou Kuenzler

I'm drawing this with a stick and swamp mud!

Chapter One

I am a hopeless witch.

Everybody says so.

Especially Aunt Hemlock. She woke me up at dawn this morning just to tell me how hopeless I am.

"Belladonna Broomstick, you are the most hopeless young witch in the whole of the Magic Realm!" she said, poking me with her long fingernails as the seven warts on the end of her nose wobbled like fat green frogs.

I don't have any warts on my nose. Perhaps that's why I'm such a hopeless witch?

No nose hair

No warts

Nose hair

Wonderful warts

Frown

Smile

Ferret smell

ME

NORMAL WITCH

If I could grow just one teeny-tiny wart, I might learn to be good at magic.

I yawned and peeped at my reflection in Aunt Hemlock's magic mirror.

"Aha!" cackled the mirror. "If it's not

Belladonna Broomstick. Just look at your big brown eyes and chocolate curls. Not a wart in sight. Pathetic. What a hopeless young witch!"

"Actually, Bella, I think you're very pretty," whispered a spider that swung down from the roof of the cave.

"Thank you," I blushed, understanding every word he'd said. Speaking animal languages is the only thing I am any good at.

Belladonna Broomstick's Magic Skills
Wand Work: HOPELESS
Spells: HOPELESS
Potions: HOPELESS
Talking to Animals: EXCELLENT!! YIPPEE!

"Quiet!" Aunt Hemlock grabbed the poor little spider by seven of his eight long legs and dunked him in her lumpy porridge.

"Let him go!" I cried.

As if by magic (which it probably was), Aunt
Hemlock's creepy chameleon,
Wane, appeared on the kitchen
shelf. Wane gives me the shivers.
I never know what colour he
is going to be or where he will appear next.
He's always spying on me and telling tales to
Aunt Hemlock. Right now he was disguising
himself behind a jar of frogspawn.

"Yum! Is that spider for me, mistress?"
he slurped, sticking out his long purple
tongue.

"Certainly not!" Aunt Hemlock dangled
the spider above her open mouth. "This one
is mine."

"Stop!" I begged, but Aunt Hemlock
swallowed the poor thing whole. "How
horrible!" I shuddered.

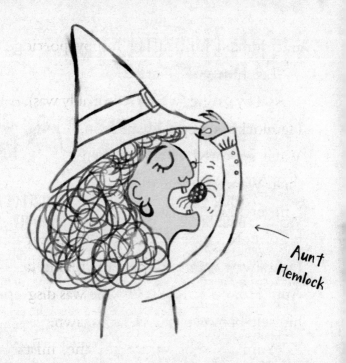

Aunt
Hemlock

"And very unfair not to share," sulked
Wane, turning piglet-pink in a huff.

Aunt Hemlock ignored us both and
picked her teeth with a chicken bone.

"You're looking marvellously magical
today, if I may say so, mistress," said the
mirror, sucking up to her as usual. . .

WORLD BOOK DAY *fest*

WORLD
BOOK
DAY
3 MARCH 2016

Want to **READ** more?

SPONSORED BY
NATIONAL
BOOK
tokens

 VISIT

YOUR LOCAL BOOKSHOP

- Get some great recommendations for what to read next

- Meet your favourite authors & illustrators at brilliant events

- Discover books you never even knew existed!

 FIND YOUR LOCAL BOOKSHOP www.booksellers.org.uk/bookshopsearch

 JOIN

YOUR LOCAL LIBRARY

You can browse and borrow from a HUGE selection of books and get recommendations of what to read next from expert librarians—all for **FREE**! You can also discover libraries' wonderful children and family reading activitie

FIND YOUR LOCAL LIBRARY www.findalibrary.co.uk

GET **ONLINE**

VISIT **WORLDBOOKDAY.COM** TO DISCOVER A WHOLE NEW WORLD OF BOOKS!

- Downloads and activities for top books and authors
- Cool games, trailers and videos
- Author events in your area
- News, competitions and new books—all in a FREE monthly email

 AND MORE!